The Tall Story

A Catalogue record for this book is available from
the British Library

ISBN 0 340 86578 4

Offset by Avon Dataset Ltd, Bidford-on-Avon, Warks

Printed in Hong Kong by
Wing King Tong

Hodder Children's Books
A division of Hodder Headline Limited
338 Euston Road
London NW1 3BH

The Tall Story

FRIEDA HUGHES

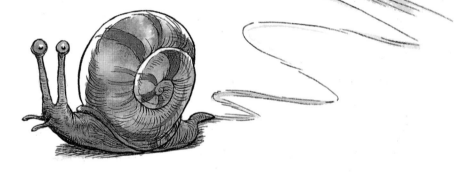

Hodder
Children's
Books

a division of Hodder Headline Limited

Chapter One

"I suppose you have a good excuse again?" sighed Mrs Williams. Micky grinned.

"Yes, Miss," he replied, "I honestly did write my story for English, but Dad accidentally used it to light the fire. He would have told you himself, but he's gone to Russia for a few days. I'll write another story by the time we come back from half-term. Promise."

"Perhaps your mother would like to confirm this when she gets back from collecting lizards in Singapore?" remarked Mrs Williams drily. "Have the story finished by the time we come back to school. This is your last chance."

Micky squirmed. He knew if he didn't have the story ready this time, he would be in trouble. But he didn't have a clue what to write about.

When he got home, Micky sneaked upstairs. "It's bath night tonight!" his mother called after him. Micky groaned.

It was such a bother to go through all that business of getting wet.

He took the hamster from the cage in his bedroom and let him out for a run on the back lawn.

"Mum," he said in a small voice, "I took William out into the garden for a minute and I lost him. It'll take me a while to find him, so can I have a bath tomorrow?"

His mother followed Micky outside.

"He went down there!" Micky said tearfully, pointing to one of the drains. There was a big piece missing out of a corner of the grate.

"Oh no!" exclaimed his mother. She called his father.

His father sighed. He lifted the grate and shone a torch into the blackness beyond.

"There is a manhole cover before the drain reaches the road," he muttered.

Micky watched in fascination as his father's head and shoulders disappeared in his efforts to get a better look. "It's disgusting down here," his father shouted from the manhole.

"Be careful dear," pleaded Micky's mother.

"I can't see William," called Micky's father. "He's probably miles away by now. Hang on, what's this?"

Micky's father reached further into the smelly, slimy drain. He emerged holding a wet, dirt-covered cloth object between his thumb and forefinger.

"I thought you said your friend Steven had borrowed the jacket your Aunt Winnie gave you for your birthday," he growled at Micky. Micky gazed at the dripping blue anorak in his father's hand.

"He did," he insisted, "I don't know how it got down the drain. Really I don't."

At that most unfortunate moment, William decided to wake up. He inconveniently climbed out of Micky's trouser pocket and fell with a light thud on to the grass at Micky's feet. There was a short, stunned silence.

"I really thought he *had* fallen down the drain, Dad," said Micky in a very small voice. He picked up the hamster. "He must have crawled back in my pocket when I wasn't looking."

"Go to your room," his father told him furiously. Micky knew he had gone too far this time. His mother had to hose the dirt from the drain off his father on the back lawn.

Chapter Two

Supper was eaten in silence.

"I suppose this isn't a good time to tell you about the giraffe at the bottom of the garden?" Micky asked quietly. His parents stared at him in disbelief.

"There really was one," he insisted. "I'm not making it up. Honest."

"I cannot believe," his mother said slowly, "that after all the trouble you caused this afternoon, you would *dare* try and tell any more stories. Go to your room again!"

Half an hour later his father followed him, sat on the edge of his bed and cleared his throat.

"Micky, your mother and I have decided it would be good for you to stay with your grandmother for a short while. You'll enjoy the sea, and maybe she can teach you something."

"Someone should feed the giraffe!" called Micky plaintively, as his father left.

Chapter Three

Micky didn't know his grandmother very well. She kept herself to herself most of the time. She was quite tall and slim, with long bony fingers and big blue eyes.

On his first night she sat him down to a dinner of chicken, potatoes and cabbage.

"Didn't Mum tell you I don't like cabbage?" he grumbled.

"If that's the way you feel, you have two choices," said his grandmother with a smile; "you can eat it so fast that it doesn't touch the sides and you don't taste it. Or you can eat it really slowly, in such small mouthfuls that you can't tell what it is."

Micky let out a sudden shout. "Aagh!" he cried. "Look! There's a huge caterpillar in the cabbage," he lied, "I can't possibly eat that!"

He was about to leap to his feet and run from the room with his hand over his mouth, but his grandmother caught him firmly by the arm and pulled him back down into his seat.

"Let's have a look, shall we?" she said calmly.

Carefully, she lifted some of his cabbage with her fork.

"Well, well," she said. "Look what we have here…" She poked her fork into the cabbagy folds and speared an impressive-looking boiled green caterpillar.

"Ugh!" groaned Micky, putting his hands over his mouth for real.

"The poor creature is quite clean," his grandmother informed him. "Full of vitamins. I ought to make you eat him!"

"You eat him!" demanded Micky rudely. His grandmother looked at him in surprise. Then she looked at the caterpillar. She bit off the head first, then finished the rest of it in two delightful mouthfuls.

"If I can eat the caterpillar," retorted his grandmother, "then I'm sure you're not such a wimp that you won't eat your cabbage."

Micky ate his cabbage.

"We'll have something a little French tomorrow," his grandmother told him. "I'm practising French cookery."

"Do they use a lot of cabbage?" Micky muttered. But she ignored him and told him to take a shower.

"I'm allergic to soap!" he protested. "Mum didn't send me with any of my special soap! I'll have to wait until we get some."

"Wash without soap," she said evenly.

Micky grudgingly did as he was told.

Of course, since he wasn't really allergic to it, he used the soap. But just as he was ready for bed, he began to itch all over. He looked in the mirror and found he was covered in a big, blotchy rash.

"Gran!" he shouted. She came running.

"I thought," she said mildly, "you were allergic to soap. You knew not to use it, didn't you?"

She rubbed some cream into his skin, and by morning he was himself again.

Chapter Four

Micky phoned his mother. "I'm bored here, Mum, I want to come home."

"Not a chance!" his mother told him. "You're staying for a while longer."

"Bored, are you?" asked his grandmother, overhearing him. She took him down to the beach for the rest of the day.

Micky waited until she got settled with her blanket, her book and her sunshade then he came running up to her shouting, "Look, look, there's a whale just offshore. Come and look."

"How wonderful!" his grandmother cried. She dropped everything and scrambled to her feet to go and see. Micky fell on the sand laughing, wondering how long it would be before she realized he was joking.

Someone further down the beach shouted "whale" and suddenly everyone else was running down to the edge of the water.

"Hey, I was only playing a joke on my gran," he called after them, but they didn't seem to hear him.

Micky went down to the water's edge to see what would happen when everyone realized it was all a hoax.

But they were already on their way back. "It was wonderful!" his grandmother told him, beaming. "What a sight!"

"What do you mean?" cried Micky.

"The whale, of course," his grandmother replied with a puzzled expression. "What did you think I meant?"

Even the people around him were talking about it. Micky ran down to the sea. He'd never actually seen a real live whale before and now he'd missed it.

Not far from shore, the sea boiled and a gigantic tail flipped beneath the froth.

That evening supper began with lettuce soup. Micky looked at it suspiciously. "I think there's a frog in mine," he said.

"Really?" asked his grandmother. With a sigh of exasperation, she took his bowl and stuck her bony fingers into it.

"I thought there was one missing!" she cried, and fished a fat frog out of his dish. It gurgled loudly, slithered out of her fingers and hopped wetly across the kitchen floor where it hid under the fridge.

"You can keep it if you like," said his grandmother. "I have all the frogs I need."

"Need for what?" Micky wanted to know. His grandmother presented him with a plate of beautifully laid out little frogs' legs.

"Pretend they're chicken," she instructed, gnawing at the ones on her own plate. "Very French," she grinned.

Then Micky complained there was a snail in his salad. He watched the salad very carefully. First there was no snail, then, suddenly, there was, its eyes swinging on the end of long stalks. Very odd.

His grandmother picked it out and popped it into a jar to become snails cooked in garlic butter some other time.

Micky phoned his best friend, Steven. "Come and visit," he begged. "It's strange staying here. Things keep happening."

"Like what?" asked Steven.

"Well," began Micky, "if I say something is real, then it becomes real."

"You mean you're not lying any more?" Steven asked in disbelief.

There was a short silence while Micky realized his best friend thought he was a liar. "Please come round," he pleaded.

Steven agreed to visit the following day.

Chapter Five

That night he told his grandmother how he and Steven had gone on a school camping holiday. How Steven had fallen and broken his leg. How he had made a stretcher out of old bits of gate and wire he found.

"Is this true?" asked his grandmother. Micky insisted it was.

He was woken in the morning by a call from Steven to say he couldn't come; he had fallen and broken his leg.

This is too much! thought Micky to himself. Everything he lied about, happened. He decided to put it to the test.

"There is a pot of gold buried in the middle of the garden," he announced out loud. Then he took a shovel from the garden shed and began to dig a hole in the middle of the lawn.

He didn't have to dig very far when the shovel chinked on something. Quickly, with his mouth dry from excitement, Micky fell to his knees and began to clear around the object he had found.

It was, indeed, a pot of gold. It glittered and shone in the sun. Micky brushed the earth off it. It was an old flower pot painted in bright gold paint. It was cracked and chipped with age.

"We might as well make that spot into a flower bed, since you've dug it all up," said his grandmother pleasantly.

Micky was so disappointed he didn't think to say "I've already done it" to see if it would get done by itself.

By the time he had made a rather nice little rose bed and had a hot bath without a single complaint, Micky was ready to fall asleep with his head in his dinner.

His grandmother looked at him kindly. "Every time you feel like telling a story," she suggested, "you should write it down instead. That way you will get to enjoy the idea of it without getting yourself into trouble."

"My story about the giraffe at the bottom of the garden isn't a made-up story," he explained to his grandmother. "It's really true. But Mum and Dad won't believe me."

"That's because everything else you tell them is rubbish," his grandmother pointed out. "But I shall tell them you haven't lied to me once since you have been here. Can I do that?" She looked at Micky searchingly.

Of course, Micky knew he'd done nothing *but* lie. He made up his mind never to tell another lie again. It was too dangerous. Well, maybe there was just *one* lie he would try. Later.

"Yes, you can tell them," he said.

He stayed for the rest of the week. On the morning he was leaving, he sneaked down to the beach on his own and sat at the water's edge with the waves licking around him. There was no one else there.

He thought about wishing for a whale, then he changed his mind.

"There is a big, grisly sea monster out there!" he whispered.

Then there it was; the sea bulged and spluttered, and a gigantic head, trailing fleshy tendrils emerged like a mountain from the heaving water. Two massive green eyes blinked at him from beneath

eyebrows like bushes. Its dark body rose out like an island. For a moment it seemed to hesitate, water pouring from between its enormous head-lumps, before the sea churned and it sank again.

"Wow!" gasped Micky.

Chapter Six

"Did you have a good stay?" his father asked when he came to collect Micky.

"Yes, and I have stopped lying," replied Micky with some pride.

"Well, we'll see how long it lasts," his father retorted.

Micky realized that it was going to take a while for his parents to trust him again.

That night, while it was all fresh in his mind, Micky wrote about his holiday with his grandmother, and how everything he said had come true. Even the sea monster, since no one was going to believe the story anyway. He would remember that sea monster for ever.

Before he went to bed he found his parents in the living-room. "Mum, Dad," he said, "there really *is* a giraffe at the bottom of the garden, you know."

"Oh no!" cried his father in mock horror, "not the dreaded giraffe again!"

Micky waited until no one was looking and sneaked out of the back door. He collected an armful of cabbages from his father's vegetable patch, which he piled by the hedge at the bottom of the garden.

He pulled a few leaves off one of the cabbages and handed them up to the huge head that lowered itself out of the sky.

A long tongue delicately wrapped around the leaves and two enormous eyes glowed at Micky with pleasure.

"I did *try* to tell them," Micky grinned at the giraffe, "but they simply won't believe me. Perhaps you could work your way through the spinach and Brussels sprouts next?"

It was the first day after half-term. Micky was astonished to see Steven at school.

"I thought you broke your leg!" he cried accusingly. Steven blushed for a moment.

"Actually," confessed Steven, "I did sprain my ankle falling downstairs." He lifted the bottom of his trousers to show he was still wearing a bandage. "But I wanted to make it sound more important, the way you would have done."

"I won't be doing that any more," promised Micky.

He handed his English story in to Mrs Williams. She glanced through it with a look of growing pleasure, then made him read it aloud to the class.

Steven was the first one to laugh, then the laughter spread. By the time Micky got to the part about the sea monster, tears were pouring down Mrs Williams' face. He looked around him in astonishment,

everyone was howling with laughter. He flushed with pleasure. So this was the way to tell a story...

"Then there was this giraffe," he told them.

These colour story books are short, accessible novels for newly confident readers